Santa's Big Smile

Charlie Alexander

Santa's Big Smile

Written by
Charlie Alexander
&
Sarah Frances Voelkel

My thanks to Kristyn Kennedy
and
Sarah Voelkel for their incredible art
work!

These two honor students attend
classes in high school.
Kristyn lives in Ocala FL.
Sarah lives in Burke VA.

Santa's Big Smile

Art Work by:

Kristyn Kennedy

Sarah Voelkel &

Charlie Alexander

Have your Elf a Merry Little Christmas!

How much did Santa's sleigh cost?

Nothing. It was on the house!

What do snowmen eat for breakfast?

Frosty Flakes!

Santa asked Mrs. Claus, "Do you think it's going to rain-dear?"

Do you know why Santa has three gardens?
So He can:

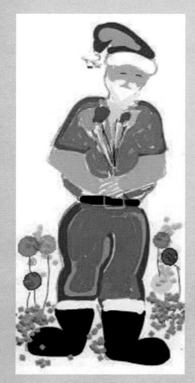  

Ho!   Ho!   Ho!

Mrs. Claus said "Hee, Hee, Hee!"

While on a secret shopping spree!

I heard Santa tell one of the Elves
to stay in the present!

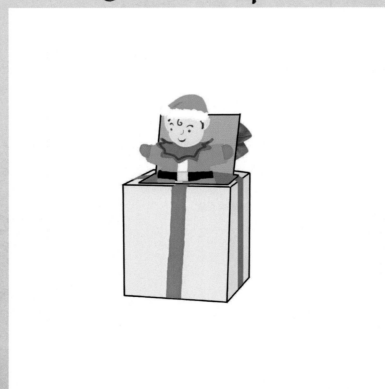

What type of music do Elves like
to listen to?

Wrap Music!

Which reindeer is the most impolite?

Rude-olf!

All Santa's helpers always feared,

They'd be chosen to trim His beard!

Which reindeer has a lot of heart?

Cupid!

Which reindeer did Santa honor?

Donner!

It's "Blitzen" who really "fits in!"

Santa learned the two step, because
he took lessons with Dancer!

Santa loves his big red hat, except when he becomes too fat!

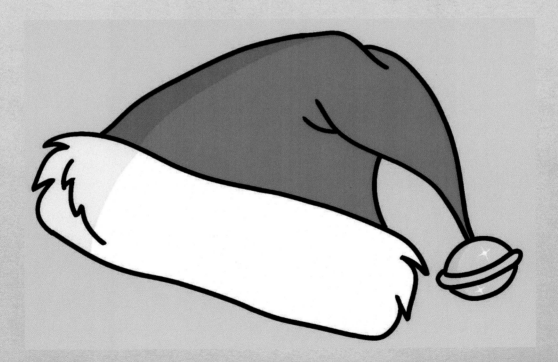

Rudolph thought it would be so nice not
to land and slide on ice!

Santa's eye glasses were lost and missed.
He had to ask Mrs. Clause to read the list!

It's not just a tease. Santa plays the keys!

How do you know Santa is real?

You can always sense His presents!

If the ride gets too bumpy, Santa just might get grumpy!

It wasn't a rumor that Santa said to quit Prancing around!

So many Christmas Eves made Santa roll up his sleeves!

Even after a thousand miles,
Santa's reindeer all wore smiles!

The Christmas batter needed mix'n.

This was a job left for Vixon

Being a reindeer named Olive is the pits!
Olivia would be nice!

The sleigh was steered by Dasher,
so Santa wouldn't crash her!

All the reindeer and Santa were proud,
as they flew very fast through a big white
cloud!

A nice cup of coffee and a delicious cookie proved that Santa wasn't a rookie!

Santa's sleigh was ready to lift.
But first He gave his Mrs. a gift!

Santa said, " only in a pinch would he call the Grinch!"

Santa and reindeer were very witty.

As they passed out gifts in every city!

While Santa was mopping the reindeer went shopping!

Don't think only of yourself,

Give a present to an Elf!

Santa sat up and was awake.

Just in time for a piece of cake!

What does Santa use to clean his sleigh?

Comet!

All the helpers were filled with glee as they decorated Santa's tree!

Mommy kissed Daddy

"Hoe, Hoe, Hoe!"

Underneath the Mistletoe!

Santa and reindeer climbed the sky,

To bring joy!
The Reason Why!

Every mile made
Santa's Big Smile!

What did the ghosts say on New Year's Eve?

Happy Boo Year!

The End

To order additional copies of this book, contact:
Xlibris
844-714-8691
www.Xlibris.com
Orders@Xlibris.com

Library of Congress Control Number: 2023907084
ISBN: Softcover   978-1-6698-7351-8
            Hardcover   978-1-6698-7355-6
            EBook   978-1-6698-7354-9

Print information available on the last page

Rev. date: 04/11/2023

Printed in the United States
by Baker & Taylor Publisher Services